Amasa Walker's
SPLENDID
GARMENT

Emily Chetkowski

Illustrated by Dawn Peterson

Alan C. Hood & Company, Inc.
CHAMBERSBURG, PENNSYLVANIA

Amasa Walker's Splendid Garment

Text Copyright © 1996 Emily Chetkowski
Illustrations Copyright © 1996 by Dawn Peterson

Published by Alan C. Hood & Co., Inc.
P.O. Box 775, Chambersburg, PA 17201

ISBN 0-911469-21-4

"Amasa Walker's Splendid Garment" was created
from a work written by Amasa Walker entitled
"Old New England Customs, Manufactures of the Household".
This paper was read to the New England Historic
Genealogical Society around 1850.

Manufactured in the United States of America

Library of Congress Control Number: 2003102318

Book design by Dawn Peterson

10 9 8 7 6 5 4 3 2 1

To Amasa,
and all the children he taught
and continues to teach.

ELC

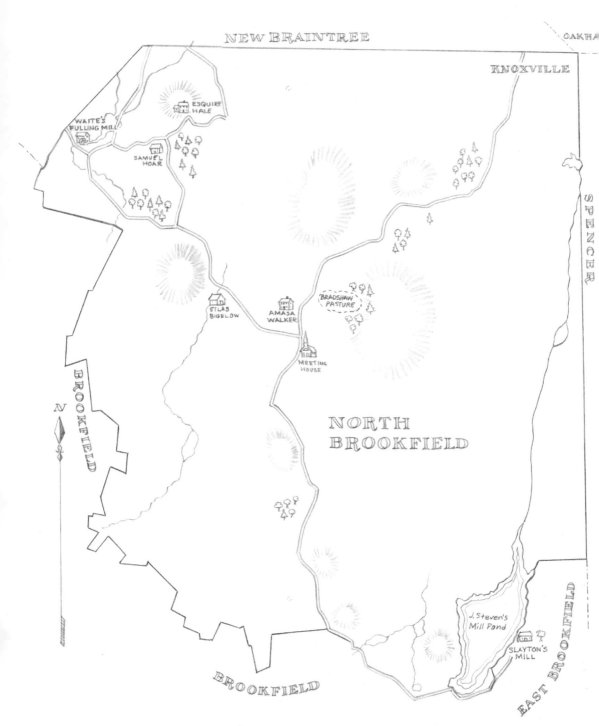

Map of Amasa's Travels

Some of the sights shown on this map are accurate and still present today,
while other locations are approximate and uncertain.

FOREWORD

Amasa Walker[1] was born on May 4th, 1799 in the village of Muddy Brook, Connecticut (now known as East Woodstock). The oldest son of Walter Walker and Priscilla Carpenter, he lived there for two years before his family moved to the North Parish of Brookfield, Massachusetts. There he attended Center District School and helped out on his father's farm, although he was a rather frail and sickly child. Unable to participate in many athletic sports, Amasa instead found great pleasure in reading and studying, which aided him in becoming a brilliant scholar.

Clothing, in Amasa's time, was very often made by the person who wore it, and a great amount of labor was involved. Garments were worn carefully, and repaired skillfully to keep them looking as new as possible. If new clothing was needed, the wool must be raised, sheared, carded, spun, woven, colored, and pressed, then cut out and sewed. It was a long and tedious process. This was especially true of a coat, as it was the handsomest garment a child could wear then, and a great deal of care went into making one. Such was the case in 1811, when it was time for a new coat for Amasa Walker.

This story is adapted from a speech that Amasa gave in the 1850s, when he was much older, and when all you had to do to get a new coat was step into a clothing store and buy one.

1—AMASA: Pronounced Am´·ah·sah

In the spring of 1811, when I was 12 years old, my mother told me she wanted to make me a new surtout[1]. She would need to get some fine wool, not Merino[2], but some fine native wool. My father, although he had a good farm, never kept sheep. He was more of a mechanic[3] than a farmer, so we had no wool. Since all the farmers employed him though, he could easily get all the wool he wanted as payment, especially now during shearing time.

My mother said, "Son, saddle Jenny and take this sheet, and go up to Mr. Silas Bigelow's to get some wool that your father has picked out. I want it for the garment we are to make for you." She had found me busy reading as was my favorite pastime, but I was all too happy to help out. You see, I had been so troubled with illness lately, that I had not been able to do many chores, but here was one I could manage. I went to the Bradshaw, (a pasture known more for its Whortleberries[4] than good hay), caught our horse Jenny, and rode her up to the house bareback. I put on the saddle and started out for Mr. Bigelow's.

1—SURTOUT: Pronounced "sir-too". A very fancy coat. It had a fitted top and a greatly flared skirt. A surtout was usually made of the finest material and best buttons.

2—MERINO: Very fine and soft wool that comes from the Merino breed of sheep.

3—MECHANIC: A person who made their living using their hands; a tradesman such as a blacksmith, cooper (barrel maker), tinsmith, printer, etc. Amasa's father was known as a blacksmith.

4—WHORTLEBERRIES: Also known as Huckleberries, the Whortleberry bush is wild and grows in thickets. It has edible berries that are similar to blueberries.

Jenny was frisky as I hadn't ridden her in a long time. I held the reins tight and she soon settled down as we traveled along. Arriving at Silas Bigelow's, I was given a huge bundle of wool. I wrapped it in the sheet mother gave me, then strapped the whole thing on the saddle behind me. It came up as high as my head and was very clumsy, though it was not very heavy. You would think a boy would look silly riding through Main Street with such a rigging[1], but it looked well enough because it was a common sight.

On the way back, Jenny wanted to gallop. I struggled to stop her, but the bundle came loose and the wool spilled out! I carefully gathered it up and picked out the leaves and dirt that had stuck to the fleece[2]. Aye, and it was no easy task catching Jenny. She wanted nothing to do with me or my bundle! I had to part with my apple in order to catch her. Then I tied on the bundle and resumed my journey. Now I was worried that Mother would be disappointed if she knew I had almost ruined the fleece, and had failed at such a simple task. I decided it was best not to mention it, and hoped my smelling like a sheep from handling the greasy wool would not make her suspicious.

1—RIGGING: Apparatus, gear

2—FLEECE: The coat of wool sheared from a sheep. It is usually done once a year and removed in one piece.

Worn out, I managed to get home without another mishap. Right away, my mother took on the role of wool stapler and sorter[1]. She picked out the tag-locks[2] and selected the best part of the fleece with which to make my coat. She didn't seem to notice the extra dirt I had added to the fleece and to myself. Watching her work, it was hard for me to imagine that the big pile of smelly wool would ever become a fashionable garment.

After a few days, (and a bit of rest), I had orders to fetch Jenny again. A large bundle was made of the wool and fastened behind the saddle as before, and I was sent on the mission of getting it carded[3]. The carding machine[4] was a wonderful new invention. It spared my busy mother the tedious task of using hand cards[5] to comb and prepare the wool for spinning[6]. So, I set off right away for the one at Slayton's Mill.

1 — WOOL STAPLER and SORTER: A person performing the task of sorting a fleece by length and quality of wool, saving the best parts for finer garments.

2 — TAG-LOCKS: The dirty unusable pieces of wool that are skirted (removed by hand) from the edges of the fleece in preparation for carding and spinning.

3 — CARDED: Fiber such as wool that has been combed before spinning. This can be done by hand, or by machine in large quantities.

4 — CARDING MACHINE: A large machine that cards wool for spinning.

5 — HAND CARDS: Wire-toothed brushes used to hand comb and prepare wool for spinning. It can be a tedious and time-consuming process.

6 — SPINNING: Twisting fibers into thread or yarn

Again I had some difficulty managing Jenny, especially when we passed a spring pasture of fresh clover. She was understandably more interested in the clover than our mission. Still, I pushed her on toward Slayton's Mill. When I arrived, Mr. Slayton was overrun with business; everybody wanted their wool carded, and his machine operated slowly. "You cannot have your rolls[1] under a fortnight[2]," said he. So I left my bundle, telling him he would find a package of lard[3] inside to use when carding the wool, and I returned home.

The fortnight passed, and I saddled up Jenny again and set off for the rolls. The road seemed longer today, but I arrived at last and asked for my wool. "Not done," said Mr. Slayton, "and it won't be for at least a week." This would be bad news for my mother, as she wished to get to work on the wool. It was bad news for me also, as I did not wish to have to travel so far again. However, there was nothing I could do about it.

1 — ROLLS: Bundles of wool that have been carded into a long, continuous roll-like form (now known as "roving") and are ready to spin.

2 — FORTNIGHT: Fourteen days; two weeks

3 — LARD: Animal fat. In this story, it was used to restore luster and softness to the wool after washing it. Wool was commonly washed with lye that cleaned it well, but made it very dry and rough. The greasy lard was applied to the wool usually the day before carding it.

As we passed that spring pasture on the way home, I decided to let Jenny graze while I did some reading. After such a disappointing trip, we both deserved a little rest, but I never expected to fall asleep! I awoke with a start when Jenny nudged me, which was a good thing. I must have been asleep a long time, as the sun was now low in the afternoon sky. It was getting late and we were far from home. I did not want to be out after dark, especially without a lantern, so we set off in haste to outrun the night.

Though Jenny was swift, it soon grew very dark and I had trouble finding my way. When we came to a fork in the road, I tried to go one way but Jenny turned to go the other. I could not change her mind, so off we went down the path she chose. I was sure we were lost. To my great relief, we soon came upon familiar sights and I realized that Jenny was right. I gave her a grateful pat on the neck. When we arrived home, my worried mother was standing in the doorway. Although she was glad to see me, Mother was not pleased with Mr. Slayton's message.

One week passed and I again returned to the carding mill. At last the work was done. The wool was put up in a huge bundle, larger than before because the rolls were so bulky. I was afraid it would spill off the saddle, especially when Jenny saw those pastures again, so I used more rope to tie it on. Perhaps Jenny remembered what happened the last time we stopped there, for this time she headed straight home. She didn't give me any trouble.

My mother was quite happy to see me arrive with the rolls, and she and the hired girl[1] were soon at work upon them. The spinning was done on the great wheel[2], for the little or foot wheel[3] was used only for spinning flax[4]. They worked diligently and I could often hear the buzz of the wheel at some distance from the house. Sometimes I could see them through the window, walking back and forth to draw out the fibers[5] while twisting and winding the yarn onto the wheel's spindle.

1 — HIRED GIRL: A girl hired to help out with the houshold tasks such as spinning, cooking or child care, etc. This arrangement may be for just one day, or she may even live in for awhile.

2 — GREAT WHEEL: or Wool Wheel. A large spinning wheel that the spinner stood beside, drawing out the long fibers with one hand while walking back and forth, and turning the wheel with the other hand.

3 — FOOT WHEEL: A small spinning wheel with a foot pedal that the spinner sits at to spin. It was traditionally used for spinning flax into linen. Also known as a Low, Saxony or Flax Wheel.

4 — SPINNING FLAX: To spin the fibers from the flax plant, from which linen cloth is woven.

5 — DRAW OUT THE FIBER: Gently pulling on and lengthening the wool as it is being spun to make it the desired thickness.

In a short time, the yarn was ready. My mother said, "Amasa, take this yarn up to Mrs. David Doane's to be woven[1] into cloth." Mrs. Doane had a loom[2] and a reputation as a very good weaver[3]. Mother had already arranged for her to do the job right away. So, with my bundle of yarn tied onto the saddle behind me, I set off to the weaver's. By now, Jenny was getting used to our little trips and was much better behaved. Instead, it was I who was impatient today. Once again, I was missing out on playing with my school friends, though this time it wasn't because I was ill. Even so, I was excited to arrive at Mrs. Doane's. She took the yarn and promised to have my cloth ready in only three weeks.

I kept busy during those three weeks, helping out on my father's farm, and maintaining my studies at Center District School. I never tired of Schoolmaster Brigham's lessons. He was my favorite teacher. In fact, I was reading a book he lent me when my mother told me it was time to go back to Mrs. Doane's. When I got there, the web was not out[1], but if I could wait, the good woman would finish it, cut it out of the loom[2] and have it ready for me. So I waited for what seemed a very long time. When at last Mrs. Doane was finished, I bound the cloth behind Jenny's saddle, and set off for home.

1 — WOVEN: Threads or yarn interlaced to make cloth.

2 — LOOM: A frame on which fibers or yarns are woven to make cloth, rugs, etc.

3 — WEAVER: A person who weaves for hire

4 — THE WEB WAS NOT OUT: The weaver had not yet reached the predetermined and marked end of the cloth, and was therefore not finished weaving.

5 — CUT IT OUT OF THE LOOM: Cut the threads to remove the finished cloth.

Upon my arrival, my mother examined the flannel[3] cloth carefully. Mother was very particular, and she found a slight defect. "Pity that the loom worked so badly in that spot," she said with regret. Otherwise, the cloth was perfect. Seeing it, I started to get excited about my new coat.

The next day, I was told that I must take the flannel, and another piece of cloth that my mother already had, up to Waite's Fulling Mills[1] to be colored and dressed[2]. Mother said it was enough cloth to make her three boys some winter clothing to go to school in. So once again I went out to the Bradshaw. I caught Jenny and saddled her, then tied on the bundle and set off.

When I arrived I asked anxiously, "How long will it take?" "Not under three weeks at the soonest," said Uncle Daniel Waite. "Can't it be done before that?" I asked. "No," said the cloth dresser, "and you may be glad to get it then!" Disappointed, I left my flannel and reported the facts to my mother when I arrived home. Mother was worried about the delay. It was getting late in the summer now, and I would be needing the warmth of my new surtout before long.

1—FLANNEL: A soft woven fabric made of wool and/or cotton.

2—FULLING MILL: Mill where woven wool cloth was washed and thickened by shrinking.

2—COLORED AND DRESSED: Dying cloth, and then brushing it with teasels (a rough bur from a plant) or brushes to raise the nap, making the cloth fuzzy, softer and smoother.

After three tedious weeks had passed, I found myself punctually on my way on Jenny's back to the fulling mill, but alas, the cloth was not done. It had been colored but not sheared or pressed[1]. "When can I have it?" I inquired. "Well, in ten days, probably," Uncle Daniel replied. So I made my way back home again and gave an account of my ill success. "Oh, those Waites are the slowest men that ever lived!" exclaimed my mother. "There is no getting work done by them in any season. However, even though everyone finds fault with them, their work when it's done is always first rate."

Ten more days passed slowly away, and I grew impatient waiting for my new surtout. In the meantime, I was told to go up to Mr. Samuel Clarke's, who lived next to the New Braintree line, and ask Aunt Debby, the tailoress[2], to make up my coat. So, I went to the Bradshaw pasture to get Jenny, but this time she stood there waiting for me. It seemed as though she too had heard my mother's request. She walked up to the house and knew right where to stand so I could put her saddle on. When we got to Mr. Clarke's, he informed me that the tailoress was at work at Esquire Hale's. I had no choice but to go there to deliver my mother's message.

1—SHEARED and PRESSED: Once the cloth had been colored and dressed, the brushed nap was sheared with scissors and then pressed with an iron.

2—TAILORESS: Seamstress, or woman who sews for hire.

Aunt Debby (she was known as Aunt to everybody) said, "I don't really know when I can come. I must stay at the Hale's for three more days, then I have a job at John Hunter's, and at Mr. Samuel Hoar's. And besides all that, I need to make up some clothing for my father's folks, for they cannot get along if I don't." She promised to come as soon as she could and would try to let us know when. I began to wonder if I would ever get a new coat, or just more saddle sores[1]!

I reported all this to my mother and she was not happy. However, no one could do the work as well as Aunt Debby Clarke, so we had to wait. Then one day my mother learned that she was at work at Mr. Hoar's, and I was dispatched there to ask whether she could now pick a day to come by. Jenny and I took another trip and found out that Aunt Debby would be ready one week from next Thursday, but only if we could come get her.

1—SADDLE SORES: A painful, tender spot on a horse or rider, caused by chafing or rubbing from a saddle.

The main thing now was to get the cloth from the Waites. Aye, but that's the rub[1], the Waites were notoriously slow. At last the time did arrive, though, and Jenny and I appeared once more at the clothiers[2]. This time I got the cloth, and bundled it to my saddle. By now I was weary of these chores. I didn't even bother to look at it. However, when Mother and I examined the cloth at home, I was overjoyed! It was unspoiled and a beautiful butternut color, so smooth and shiny. I had never seen anything so nice! I thought, "What a splendid garment it will make and how fine I shall look in it." Now we had only to wait for Aunt Debby.

When the day to get Aunt Debby finally came, I set off at sunrise. My fingers ached from the cold of that frosty morning. The journey seemed so long and the cold weather made me worry that my coat might not be ready when I would really need it. Jenny remembered the way to Mr. Clarke's and was as happy as I to finally arrive there. Unfortunately, Aunt Debby wasn't quite ready to leave. "I must baste[3] a garment for my sister to work upon, and cut out a jacket for Bill Watson." So I waited, but was thankful I wouldn't have to make the trip again, and the wait was not too long.

1—AYE, BUT THAT'S THE RUB: or "that's the problem"

2—CLOTHIER: One who makes or sells cloth or clothing.

3—BASTE: Loosely hand-sewing fabric together with long temporary stitches while fitting or making adjustments. Then the cloth would be permanently sewed, and the basted stitches removed. Though it is more time-consuming, it serves a similar purpose as pinning the cloth, but is easier to work with and usually produces better results.

Her work being at last finished, the good tailoress rigged up[1], got her goose iron[2] and all the necessary accessories, then put on her gloves. I brought Jenny up to the horseblock[3], and with a sort of slide and jump, Aunt Debby got on behind. She put one arm around me to hold on. This time, it seemed only a short while before Jenny and I arrived home, with our most precious cargo.

Mother was all prepared for the business at hand. The room had been cleared for action and the table was drawn out with my beautiful cloth spread upon it. Aunt Debby got out her great shears[4] and thimble[5] and mother brought out her pressing board[6]. They talked at great length about the plans for my coat: How shall it be cut, lined, and trimmed? How long shall it be? What style will the collar be, and the width of the cuffs? These were all very important matters. Aunt Debby was not certain about a few things, and discussed them very seriously, but when the talks ended, the work began.

1—RIGGED UP: Packed up

2—GOOSE IRON: A non-electric iron with a handle shaped like a goose's neck. It was heated in the fireplace and used to press cloth.

3—HORSEBLOCK: Usually made of stone, it was used as a step when getting onto a horse.

4—GREAT SHEARS: Sewing scissors

5—THIMBLE: A cap or cover worn on the end of the finger while sewing and used to help push the needle through, while protecting the finger.

6—PRESSING BOARD: Ironing board

First, Aunt Debby measured my height and width, looking through her spectacles[1] very curiously. Mother watched anxiously, all the while offering her advice and suggestions. When the measurements were completed, the critical process of cutting the cloth began. There could be no errors. Looking very serious, responsible, and maybe a bit cross (though she never looked good-natured), Aunt Debby slowly and carefully finished cutting the cloth. I remembered all those tiring trips Jenny and I had made to get to this point, and I felt very relieved that no mistakes were made.

Now they began the tedious task of making up[2] the garment; Aunt Debby basted and mother hand sewed[3]. They worked non-stop all day and all evening, until my younger brothers and I, who were constantly looking on, were sent off to bed. Walter and Freeman fell right to sleep, but I hardly slept that night thinking about my new coat.

1—SPECTACLES: Eyeglasses

2—MAKING UP: Putting together

3—HAND SEWS: Sewing cloth together using only a needle and thread. Most Early American women were skilled at and capable of intricate needlework, and were taught at a young age.

The next day they continued basting and sewing my coat, stopping every so often to have me try it on. Were the sleeves the right length? Were they too large? Was the coat too long? All these points were discussed at length, then I was sent off while they continued to work. It seemed to take forever, which worried Mother. It was near Thanksgiving, and she needed at least a week to prepare for that important holiday. Making this coat was taking up a lot of her precious time.

At long last they called for me. The great undertaking was achieved. The coat was completed. I wondered, "How will it fit?" Aunt Debby herself placed it upon me. She knew how that ought to be done for the very first time—how the collar should be pulled up and and the skirt pulled down. "There," she exclaimed proudly, "the fit is perfect; don't you think so, Mrs. Walker; don't you think so, Amasa?" Mother was so pleased, and praised Aunt Debby. I looked in the mirror, and thought, "Yes, yes; it is perfect!"

"Now, my son, get the mare as soon as can be, and carry Miss Clarke home,"said Mother. "You know she is in a great hurry." So I saddled Jenny for my final task. Aunt Debby again put her arm around me to hold on, and we made our way to the northern boundary of town as fast as possible.

Fortunately for me, the proud owner of a new surtout, the following day was Sunday. It was a beautiful day, too, and all the boys and girls were out to meeting—a perfect opportunity for me to exhibit my new coat. As we entered the churchyard, I sat tall in Jenny's saddle and felt like a handsome young man in my splendid garment. The fact that I had waited six months for it was not very unusual, but I was so proud and happy as I marched up to the front door of the old church. I deserved to be. After all, it was I who had made the thirteen journeys and traveled over eighty miles on Jenny's back, and it was I who had seen the toil and labor of love it took to make my coat, enough so that I truly understood its value.

The End

AFTERWORD

Though troubled by ill health most of his life, Amasa Walker went on to become a highly respected and prominent man. He was physically and intellectually active up until October 29, 1875, the day he peacefully and unexpectedly died only four months after his wife Hannah. Amasa was said to have enjoyed his later years the most, but his entire life was very interesting.

As a young man, he worked in the Brookfield area at various stores and was known as a diligent and faithful employee. He soon became a partner in a store in West Brookfield for three years, and made a sizeable profit when he sold out his interest.

In 1817, Amasa prepared for admission to Amherst College but was unable to continue due to poor health. For the next few years he taught school and worked on his father's farm. After entering into business in Boston as Carleton & Walker, Amasa married his partner's sister Emeline. Unfortunately, Emeline died two years later, along with their infant daughter. He later married Hannah Ambrose in 1834. They had three children, Emeline, Robert Walter, and Francis Amasa.

Amasa became involved in many political, social, and intellectual interests. In 1829, he helped form the Boston Lyceum, an organization that gave public lectures. In the same year, he became active in the movement against Masonry. He later became director of the

Franklin Bank and the Western Railroad, and president of the Boston Temperance Society. In 1842, he went to Oberlin, Ohio, to financially support and organize a college, and over the years delivered lectures there on political economy. All the while, Amasa wrote and spoke freely in support of the antislavery movement.

He returned to the family home in North Brookfield in 1843, but went to England right away as a delegate to the First International Peace Congress. Mr. Walker spent a large part of the next few years promoting international peace while residing in North Brookfield.

In 1848, he was active in forming the Free Soil Party, an antislavery organization. Shortly thereafter, he held a seat in the Massachusetts House of Representatives and became the Free Soil and Democratic candidate for Speaker of the House. He was elected to the Massachusetts State Senate and took his seat in 1850. While in the Senate, Mr. Walker passed a bill that called for Webster's Dictionary being introduced into Massachusetts schools.

He served as Massachusetts Secretary of the State for the next few years, and Secretary of the Massachusetts Board of Agriculture. He also received an honorary Master of Arts degree from Middlebury College, along with an appointment to Harvard University as an examiner of political economy. He later lectured on the subject at Amherst College. A member of the Convention for revising the Constitution of Massachusetts, he also chaired the committee on suffrage.

In 1857, Amasa Walker began publishing a series of articles on political economy in *Hunt's Merchants Magazine*. Because of his progressive views, he was immediately recognized as a leading authority on finances and was a much sought after writer and lecturer.

As a member of the Electoral College of Massachusetts, and a strong supporter of antislavery, it was Amasa's great honor to vote for Abraham Lincoln. Two years later, he was elected a Representative in Congress.

Amasa published an important book on economics, *The Science of Wealth*, of which there were eight editions, including one in Italian, and a student's version. He received a Doctor of Law degree from Amherst College in 1867, and wrote regularly for magazines such as *Lippincott's Magazine* of Philadelphia, and various newspapers up until the time of his death.

Amasa and Hannah, his wife and companion of more than forty years, frequently traveled to such places as Boston, New Haven, Washington, Florida, and even California. Wherever he went, Amasa quickly and easily made friends. He enjoyed meeting new people and participating in stimulating conversation. A graceful and distinguished man, he had a rich and powerful voice that easily captured his audience's attention.

Very fond of giving advice, Honorable Walker most enjoyed telling stories to the young about his childhood and school days, and about the early times and people of North Brookfield. Today, more than a century after he lived, Amasa Walker continues to tell a story.

AMASA WALKER—Born May 4th, 1799; died October 29th, 1875; age 76.

WALTER WALKER (Amasa's father)—Died December 14th, 1835.

PRISCILLA WALKER (Amasa'a mother)—Died October, 1835: age 60.

SILAS BIGELOW—Died October 23rd, 1820; age 44.

DAVID DOANE—Died May 19th,1816; age 71.

HANNAH DOANE (wife of David)—Died 1826.

UNCLE DANIEL WAITE—Born April 25th, 1781; died August 11th, 1856; age 75.

MISS DEBORAH CLARKE—Died June 6th, 1822; age 43.

SAMUEL HOAR—Died February 28th, 1817; age 74.

WALTER WALKER (Amasa's brother)—Born March 28th, 1801; died July 29th, 1838; age 37.

FREEMAN WALKER (Amasa's brother)—Born December 12, 1803; died July 13th, 1883; age 79.

BIBLIOGRAPHY

Kalman, Bobbie. *Children's Clothing of the 1800s*. Crabtree Publishing, 1995.

Kalman, Bobbie. *18th Century Clothing.* Crabtree Publishing, 1993.

Kalman, Bobbie. *19th Century Clothing.* Crabtree Publishing, 1993.

Larkin, Jack. *Children Everywhere.* Old Sturbridge Village booklet series, 1991.

Temple, J.H. *History of North Brookfield.* Town of North Brookfield, 1887.

Walker, Amasa. *Old New England Customs, Manufactures of the Household.* A paper read by Honorable Amasa Walker before the New England Genealogical Society, circa 1850.

ACKNOWLEDGEMENTS

A Special Thank You to:

Mary Ellen Radziewicz, who first told me about Amasa Walker.

Connie Small, Jeannette Howland, and Cynthia Kennison, of the New Braintree and North Brookfield Historic Societies, who share a fondness for Amasa, and made my research enjoyable.

Jean Contino of Old Sturbridge Village, for all her helpful information.

The American Horticultural Society, for helping me define the perplexing "Whortleberries".

John, Marek, and Hannah Chetkowski, for their patience and advice.

And to Honorable Amasa Walker, for sharing his story.

Emily Chetkowski

INDEX